FOREWORD BLESSING

Greetings in the Glorious Name of Jesus Christ, I pray your Holy Spirit fall upon your people all across this nation. Help us to praise you with all of our heart, mind, spirit and soul. Help us to be in your Holy Will, Oh God, please, I ask of thee, dear Lord!

I lift up your holy name forever, dear Father! You are my rock of salvation, the love of my life, my armor and shield of protection, Oh Lord! I just want to be pleasing in your eye sight. Please help me to be, Father. You are everything because you have all that we need, and I thank and praise you for that.

Thank you for first loving me and for seeing something in me that I did not see in myself. You saw the very best in me and I thank you for that. Thank you for accepting me when people rejected me. I know that my future is in your hand, Oh Lord! Thank you for your plan in helping me get through this journey. I am humbly thankful and grateful.

Lord, you are always in my spirit because the Bible says that the Spirit is willing, but the flesh is weak. So with that being said, when we are not praising and worshipping you in the natural, our spirit will be.

Thank you for my talent, potential and bright mind, Oh Lord. Thank you for a praying spirit for it has kept me in perfect peace. Thank you for the fence of protection you have placed around me and my loved-ones. Thank you for your angels you assigned to watch over us as we go on our everyday activities.

Truly you bring out the best in me. I thank you for working on me slowly but surely.

I love you with all that's within me, Oh Lord!!!!

Nira Saleh

CONTENTS

~

LOVER'S ROCK

BOOK OF PRAYERS AND POEMS

PRAYERS

© "THANK YOU FOR UNCONDITIONAL LOVE"
©
by Nira M. Saleh

Dear Lord,

First of all, I want to say, "Greetings Father". I thank you for the opportunity to stand humbly before your Throne of Grace right now to say, "Thank You"!

Oh Lord, you are the love song that's in my heart and it's so amazing, you are so great, Oh Father!

If it was not for your grace and mercy, I don't know where I would be, dear Lord! Truly you bring out the best in me. And for this I am truly thankful and grateful; unto thee.

Oh Father, thank you for your unconditional love that you have towards us each and every single day. I am so thankful unto you!

Love ya!!!!

© "ALL PRAISES GO TO YOU" ©
by Nira M. Saleh

Dear Lord,

I just want to thank you for you being yourself at all times, and for that I am truly thankful and grateful unto thee, Oh Lord! Thank you for your so many blessings, big and small. Thank you for always thinking of me.

All praises go to you, Oh Lord! Thank you for your grace and mercy that you show toward us daily. I love you with all I have in me.

Amen

© "LORD, I'M RETURNING BACK TO YOU" ©
by Nira M. Saleh

Oh Heavenly Father, I take this time now to say,

Thank You, Oh God!

I thank you for always bring there for me.

Oh Lord, I know that many of times I strayed away, but Lord,

I'm returning back to you.

You have been so patient and so kind.

Truly Heavenly Divine, in what other way could I make you

proud than to rededicate my life to you?

For your love was always so true.

Oh Lord, I love you with everything I have within me.

Your love has truly set me free. I'm returning back to you.

For I owe you my life.

In many ways you spared my life so I take this moment to

rededicate my all to you, Lord.

I'm returning back to you for I know that I can never

repay you, but I offer you the best I have.

I love you, Dear Lord!

© "LORD, I'M LOOKING FOR A TURNAROUND" ©
by Nira M. Saleh

Lord, I'm looking for a turnaround within me that

will make you proud, Oh Lord. I'm looking

for a turnaround in my mind, heart, body, and spirit, Oh Lord.

I'm looking to grow spiritually in faith. I ask that you will help

me to increase in you, Oh Lord, and decrease in myself

because if I decrease in myself, there would be room

to grow in Jesus, Oh Lord!

I truly want to be used of God so that the glory of God

will be glorified through your holy name, Oh Lord!

I'm looking for a turnaround that will shake the Devil's

playground. I want to be unstoppable through the spirit of the

Lord. I want to grow stronger in all areas of my life.

Help me to stay in your holy will.

Dear Lord, I'm looking for a turnaround,

not only for me but for the world to see.

And, most of all, for you, Oh Lord!

© "ANOTHER DAY'S JOURNEY"©
by Nira M. Saleh

Dear Lord,

I just want to start by saying, thank you for another day's journey. I truly thank you, Oh God for your so many blessings day-in and day-out.

Oh Father, thank you for waking me up this morning and starting me on my way. I thank you for last night's rest and for this, I am truly thankful and grateful unto thee, Oh Lord.

Thank you for your unconditional love that you show towards me daily. Thank you for life, health, and strength. Thank you for my family, friends and loved-ones that are in my life. Thank you for all things.

Amen

© "HEAVENLY FATHER" ©
#1
by Nira M. Saleh

Dear Heavenly Father,

I come to you now with an open heart and a sound mind, Oh Lord. I thank you, Oh God for waking me up this morning and starting me on my way, and for that I am truly grateful unto thee! I thank you for last night's rest and another opportunity to say thank you for all that you have done, going to do, and for being just who you are.

Lord, I thank you for grace and mercy and I praise you with all that I have within me. I thank you for the strength to carry on each and every day and for the faith to believe in a higher power in which is in your Holy Spirit, Oh Lord! Help me to hold on to your unchanging hands, Dear Lord!

I rededicate myself back to you, Oh Lord. Please accept me into your arms of grace and mercy. Thank you for bringing about a change within me and for being there for me each and every day, Oh Lord!

I love you, Oh Lord with all I have in me.

Amen

© "HEAVENLY FATHER" ©
#2
by Nira M. Saleh

Dear Lord,

I thank you for having grace and mercy toward me this morning and starting me on my way. Thank you for last night's rest and for that I am truly thankful and grateful unto you.

Oh God, thank you for another day's journey. I come to you now, yet I am not worthy to stand before your throne of grace. I am so grateful to you, Oh Lord.

Help me to stand in that day of the Lord. I want and need to be ready for the coming of the Lord! Please help me to be ready, Oh Lord! Help me to keep my mind stayed on you at all times.

I love with all I have in me, Dear Lord.

Amen

© "THANK YOU, OH LORD" ©
#1
by Nira M. Saleh

Dear Lord,

Thank you for grace and mercy and your unconditional love you give us each day, Oh Lord! Thank you for the faith to believe and trust in you. I need you in my life every day whether things are good or bad. Oh Father, please help me to be what you would want me to be. Please give me a spirit of praise deep down in my soul.

Dear Lord, you are the reason why I live each and every day. Oh Father, Oh God, please help me to be better for you and for myself.

I thank you each day, Oh Father! I love you, Oh Lord each day more and more.

Amen

© "THANK YOU, OH LORD" ©
#2
by Nira M. Saleh

Dear Father,

Help me, Oh Lord, to be more like you each day and to get closer to the Kingdom of God. Help me to be used by you in every way, Dear Father, I ask of you. I want to dwell in your holy presence!

Oh Lord, pour out your Holy Spirit on all flesh, I ask of Thee! I pray for peace, deliverance, joy, growth in you, Oh Lord, saving power, and just to do your holy will, Oh Lord!

Thank you, Oh God, for grace and mercy you show toward me each and every day of my life. Thank you for the mind to run on in this race. I love you with all I have in me, Oh Lord!

Amen

© "THANK YOU, OH LORD" ©
#3
by Nira M. Saleh

Dear Lord,

Thank you for waking me up this morning and starting me on my way. Thank you for last night's rest and for your many blessings big and small. I love them all!

Oh Lord, I just want to take this time to say thank you for another day's journey. I would like to ask that you pour out your spirit on all flesh. Lord, let your spirit saturate this place. I ask that you take out anything that is not like you within me, Oh Father. Cleanse me! Purge me! Help me to be pleasing in your eyesight, Oh Lord, I ask of Thee.

Help me to think holy thoughts at all times. Help me to sing a new song of praise deep down in my heart. Help me to stay holy in all I say and do, Oh Lord. Please let others see the God in me, and most of all, help me to get better for thee.

People will have their thoughts of me, but Lord it's what you think of me. Help me to be concentrated on you. Let us stand together in prayer, Oh Father! Please help us to return back to you. Please help us to seek after righteousness. I love you, Oh Lord, with all I have within me.

Amen

© "THANK YOU, OH LORD" ©
#4
by Nira M. Saleh

Dear Lord,

Thank you for your love, grace and mercy that you show to us each and every day of our lives. I just want to be next to you, dear Lord. Lord, I praise you with my whole heart. Help me to always have a clean heart.

You are the center of my joy. My spirit thirsts after you. Truly it does! Oh Lord, I need a deliverance from the inside to the outside. You are truly amazing. Please give me a worship experience like never before. Oh Lord, I love you and I praise you. Thank you for restoring me.

Amen

© "THANK YOU, OH LORD" ©
#5
by Nira M. Saleh

Dear Lord,

Thank you, Oh Lord, for all that you do. Thank you for waking me up this morning and starting me on my way. For that, I am truly grateful and thankful unto thee. Oh Lord, thank you for last night's rest, for your holy angels camping all around me, and for protecting me all the way. Thank you for your mercy and grace and for this, Oh Lord, I am truly grateful and thankful unto thee.

Thank you, Dear Father, for your saving power, for you are so worthy to be praised. I truly thank you! I love you with all my heart!

Amen

© "THANK YOU, OH LORD" ©
#6
by Nira M. Saleh

Dear Lord,

You are so amazing to me, Oh gracious Father! I love you with all that I have within me, Oh Lord! You brighten up my day. You have carried me through the test of all times and I'm thankful and grateful unto thee, Oh Father!

You keep me in perfect peace, Oh God, and I thank you for that. I thank you for your grace and mercy that you show towards me. That unconditional love that you show towards me is so wonderful!

Oh Lord, I thank you for uplifting my spirits in a way that I can feel my spirits to soar. I thank you for this and so much more.

Dear Lord, I thank you!!

Amen

© "THANK YOU, OH LORD" ©
#7
by Nira M. Saleh

Dear Lord,

Thank you, Oh Lord, for you being yourself at all times. I want to say thank you for last night's rest and this morning's rising. I truly thank you, Oh Lord, for your so many blessings that you bestow on us each day. How amazing you are! No one can do the things that you do. No one is like you!

Thank you for your awesome power to save, heal, and deliver, Oh Father! There is power in your holy name. Truly there is something great about the name of Jesus! For all praises belong to you. You are worthy of all praise, glory and honor.

Amen!

© "THANK YOU, OH LORD" ©
#8
by Nira M. Saleh

Dear Lord,

I truly thank you for all that you have done for me and all that you are going to do! Oh Lord, I thank you for making a way out of no way. I truly thank you for your sweet tender mercies that you continue to show me and others across the earth.

Thank you for being a bridge over troubled waters, for waking me up this morning and starting me on my way, Dear Father. Thank you for last night's rest and for this, I am truly thankful and grateful unto thee, Oh Lord!

Thank you for your protection that you constantly pro0vide for me and others. I love you, Oh Lord.

Amen

© "THANK YOU, OH LORD" ©
#9

by Nira M. Saleh

Dear Lord,

I come now, yet I am unworthy of your grace and mercy.
Thank you for the opportunity to say, "Thank You!" Lord, you
were there from the beginning and I know that you will be there
during my end. I thank you for your so many blessings, for last
night's rest and this morning's rise. For this, oh Lord, I am truly
thankful and grateful unto thee.

Oh Lord, thank you for your saving power and deliverance. You
are my peace and my provision. You carry me all the day long.
Thank you for the strength to carry on each and every single day
of my life.

You have all that I need and I thank you for being a very present
help in the time of need. I desire to dwell in your presence always
and forever. You are the "Love of my Life", Oh Father! Thank
you for your sweet spirit and for making a way out of no way. I
give you a praise from deep within my heart, Oh Father.

Father, thank you for your protection for us and our family,
friends and loved-ones. Thank you for your peacemakers for
they shall be called the children of God! Thank you for a spirit
to press forward in you and for breaking every chain of bondage
for those chains kept me from going forth, but I know that it is
revival in you, Oh Lord. And I am truly thankful and grateful
unto you!!

Thank you for your genuine spirit, Oh Lord, for it was thee, Father, who carried me through each and every day. I am asking that I would dwell in your presence forever for it will keep me in perfect peace.

Please help me to do your will, Oh Lord. I ask that you make me over again and take out anything that is not like you. Please help me to be where you are, I ask of thee.

Lord, let your Holy Spirit fall upon your people all across this nation. Help us to praise you with all of our heart, mind, spirit and soul. Help us to be in your Holy Will, Oh God, please, I ask of thee, dear Lord!

I lift up your holy name forever, dear Father! You are my rock of salvation, the love of my life, my armor and shield of protection, Oh Lord! I just want to be pleasing in your eye sight. Please help me to be, Father. You are my everything because you have all that we need, and I thank and praise you for that.

Thank you for first loving me and for seeing something in me that I did not see in myself. You saw the very best in me and I thank you for that. Thank you for accepting me when people rejected me. I know that my future is in your hand, Oh Lord! Thank you for your plan in helping me get through this journey. I am humbly thankful and grateful.

Lord, you are always in my spirit because the Bible says that the Spirit is willing, but the flesh is weak. So with that being said, when we are not praising and worshipping you in the natural, our spirit will be.

Thank you for my talent, potential and bright mind, Oh Lord. Thank you for a praying spirit for it has kept me in perfect peace.

Thank you for the fence of protection you have placed around me and my loved-ones. Thank you for your angels you assigned to watch over us as we go on our everyday activities.

Truly you bring of the best in me. I thank you for working on me slowly but surely.

I love you with all that's within me, Oh Lord!!!!

Amen

POEMS

© "THE LOVE BOX" ©
By Nira M. Saleh

This here is for the grown and sexy words that will
get you ready to express that special love
for that special someone.
It is something that will make your heart
throw or ever skip a beat.

A love so good it will sweep you off your feet. I know
what you are thinking, oh sweet, how sweet,
or how neat! I know right?

A love that will carry you through the night
while your lover holds you tight and what I
add to that; that is more than alright. I ______!

So, sit back and take a seat, it's about to flow hard and heavy so
get ready. 5,4,3,2 and 1 to blast off!
I'm about to knock your socks off, or maybe get your
rocks off. The love box holds a lot of memories, and it helps
them to see if love is expressed the right way. And, it will meet
you at heart evenly and truthfully.

The Love Box will have you sweating and begging for more.
So baby close the door and tell me your deepest
and wildest fantasy. Baby, I know that you are so
delighted to listen at you express yourself in
a way that no one can express, but you.

My Love, I hope that all your fantasies come true,
only for you. This is no longer a dream.
Baby, speak to me. I want to feel you next to me.

I want you to breathe me. The Love box has a lot of roles
which one will you play? Husband and wife,
Mistress and secret lovers, the choice is yours. There is
so many to choose from and etc., but whatever gets your
heart to beating, "yes, it's what I'm seeking!

My love, this for real. We have done all the talking and we

have done all the foreplay. Now, hold my hand
and tell me that it is okay, wait, wait, baby you are worth the
wait. You touch me here and I will touch me here
and I will touch you there.

The beast stepped out of man and he said, "You can touch me
anywhere, but the Love Box.
Because if you enter, there will be a caution sign stating
"ENTER", if you dare, so, please beware.

And tell that special love that if they're good, they are stuck
with you. Baby, I'm not that easy to cut loose, but if this is not
your destination, you can leave, if you choose.

It's not like I have some type of voodoo over you. So let's do
what we must do. This is done all in the name of love and all
because of you.

And, NO, I'm not playing! Do you hear the words I am saying?
There will be a request for more.
But, can you blame it? The Love Box is who to blame.
A love so sweet, tender, and heated. It will have you calling
your lover's name.

The Love Box, don't stop, don't stop! You are
like Folgers, good down to the last drop. Now baby stop

and get some sleep, though we'd be at it again.

This love beast has just starred. There is no need to pretend.
After a while of this, it has turned into a habit. Your loving is
so good, baby. You know I gotta have it.

One heartbeat, two heartbeats, three heartbeats, then, it's more.
You are who my soul loves and adores. Now give me more.
Honey, I'm now just trying to even the score. You have now
reached the Love Box.

© "LOVE SAVED ME" ©
by Nira M. Saleh

To get to this point in life and to acknowledge
that we are only saved by grace and mercy, in which only God
can give, I take this time to thank God for the opportunity to
live, to love, to share, to grow
and so much more.

Lord, you are who I truly adore.
I was once so hurt by the emotions of love and I knew that it
took love to get me through.
Because when someone hurts you, the best thing to remember is
to pray through the good and bad times.
God will get you through any trial and through any test.

For God's love is the best. God also forgives us of all sin.
He will truly cleanse you deep within.
Also as believers, we are to follow the same
instructions and guide.

God will lead you through the night and no one but God
can make things right.
I know that love saved me.
Look at me.
Now I'm free.

© "LOVE, WATCH OUT NOW" ©
by Nira M. Saleh

I'm so excited and highly delighted!
Overjoyed and head-over-hills!
I'm willing to take this walk with you, my love.

We're reaching higher ground, higher levels, and higher dimensions. WOW! Look out now! Reaching areas that could not be reached.

Teaching lessons never taught, listening to sermons never preached. WOW! Look out!

For this is love. Watch out now. It will show you how to walk, to cherish, to talk, to pray, to share, to respect, to honor, to give reverence, to love, to obey, and how to act. What to say, yes, I have yielded.

Love showed me how to be healed. Love, watch out now! The soft touches from my head to my toes. My love who knows where this love thang goes.

All I know is that it shows and it grows. WOW! Love, watch out now, we are reaching our peak to levels you can only seek. WOW! Love, Watch Out Now!

© "MY SUNSHINE" ©
by Nira M. Saleh

My Sunshine!
Do you hear me beloved, when I call out your name?

My Sunshine!
As I cried for the love I had for thee, I talked to the heavens and
declared that we were meant to be.

My sunshine!
We connected on a level like no other.
May I say that you are a blessing,
my brother,
my love,
my honey
and a close friend.
I will always love you until the end.

My Sunshine!
You stepped up when I backed down.
You turned my frown into a smile.

My sunshine!
I love you. So what more can I say?
I hope that this love is forever blessed of God,
Today,
Tomorrow,
and forever more.

My Sunshine!

© **"RUNNING THRU MY MIND"** ©
by Nira M. Saleh

Thinking of us how we've been thru so much.
Being in situations and wondering how we were going to
make it thru.
Oh Lord, I know it's all because of you how our love has stood
the test of all times.
But there are still things that are running
thru my mind how long will it last, how to make it better, what
will I have to sacrifice?

What's next but those questions should always make me thirst
and hunger for more of you.
Baby, maybe it's just the things you do.

You have my mind just running like I'm in a race.
You know I'm trying to win it because if I put forth this much
effort and don't win, oh well, that's life.

We can't always win and we won't always lose.
Sometimes it's in the things we choose.
WOW!
WOW!
WOW!
So much is running thru my mind.

© "LET'S CELEBRATE LOVE" ©
by Nira M. Saleh

Love!
That wonderful feeling!
To be loved
To grow in love
To share love
To walk in love
To increase in love in all areas
It's wonderful to have something so great and it doesn't cost a
thing.
Love can save
Love can heal
Love can cover a wounded heart
Love can protect
Love can open a lot of opportunities
Love is assurance
Love cannot be unsure
Love is a feeling of safety.
In love?
Let's go all the way.
Turn up!
Not stopping until you get enough.
Express it until it makes you happy.
Let it take your mind unto another place and give it all you got.
Let's celebrate love for it being just what it is nothing added
and nothing taken away. Let's step in the name of love and let
it lead the way.

Trust in it. You will be okay. Let's hold up our champagne
glasses and claim our love to be lived out loud. So declare it
now. Let's celebrate love the fullest because it is how we do
this and we are not new at this so, let's celebrate love.

© "THE BEAUTY OF TRUE LOVE" ©
by Nira M. Saleh

The beauty of True Love
The beauty of True Love
That's what I'm in need of, True Love.
That good heart felt feeling of love
In how it makes us happy with a smile from deep within the
inside that shows on the outside.
That can last for a long while.

It's enduring and everlasting and also satisfying.
A love so dear and so sweet
A love so good it is knee-deep
heart-throbbing, head bottling, over joyed.
A high love drive that will take you to the 5th gear, then to
overdrive.

Then slow down to unwind is simply amazing.
In itself that it needs nothing else to make it complete.
A love so intensifying that it will sweep you off your feet.
Then sit back and think of it. Oh, how sweet is this love?
A love that I am in the need of. The Beauty of True Love.

© "FROM THE BOTTOM OF MY HEART" ©
by Nira M. Saleh

My love, you know that I love you.
There is no one above you, but God above.
My love, sine we've been together, I see you differently
than I used to see you from the first time we met.

It is a day that I won't ever regret, my love.
Each test, each trial, and each situation that we have
been through, the lore I panicked.
The more you said I love you, and we would make it
through.
Those very words have stood by me when everything
failed. Your love lifted me and directed me in the right
direction.

Oh God, thank you for your protection my love.
I love you from the bottom of my heart to the
depths of my soul.
I asked the Lord to please take full control and
grab a hold of us forever.
Always to make us, mode us and help
our love to last for eternity.
That would be a dream to me from the bottom of my
heart.

© "LORD, PLEASE MEND THE BROKEN PIECES" ©
by Nira M. Saleh

Lord, being in situations time and time again,

I am ready to start all over again.

Oh God, I have messed up enough times

and now I am asking,

Lord, please mend the broken pieces

in my life, Oh Father.

Lord, I hoped and prayed that your Holy Will would be done in

my life, through your Son Jesus

Christ.

Please turn my wrongs into rights.

For I know who carried me from then to now.

Oh Lord, I am asking for you to show me how to go forward in

you because I only want to please you.

Lord, please mend the broken pieces.

One important key is to have faith, trust and believe.

Then in faith, receive it and know that the situation of yesterday

would be a thing of the past.

For God's love is a promise.

It will always last.

© **"WE BELONG TOGETHER"** ©
by Nira M. Saleh

We now have been together for some years.
And through our worst fears and with many tears, we have
always made it through tough situations.

We were built for this. We laughed, we cried, and in times, we
asked why. But honey, I know that we belong together.

Always and forever, we belong together. No one can make
Me happy as well as you, and no one can make me smile like
you do.

You are that fresh breath of air that I need each and every day.
I love you without a question in my mind.

I love the way you kiss me, caress me, and hold me from
behind.
My love, I am glad to say that you are mine to love,
to honor, and to cherish.

Being with you my wish is now a reality.
My love for you is complete, truly indeed.

We belong together!

© "TEACH ME YOUR WAYS"©
by Nira M. Saleh

Oh Lord, teach me your ways.

For my ways are not your ways, and your thoughts

are not my thoughts.

I desire to go higher in you and decrease

in my selfish ways and within myself.

If I increase in you, Oh Lord, I will always seek

for improvement within myself. For the

Kingdom of God is at hand for

all believers who rest and believe in God.

Oh Father, teach me your ways for you are all that I need

to survive in this life and in the next.

Oh Lord, teach me your ways, for a mind

in you will bring all hope alive. Help me to be

pleasing in your eyesight, for your love,

grace, mercy, joy, faith, hope, peace, understanding, and etc.

will guide me through with light.

Oh Lord, teach me your ways, for your ways will prepare

me for the Master's use. I only want to

be used of you.

Oh Lord, teach me your ways!!

© "TICKLED BY LOVE" ©
by Nira M. Saleh

Great thoughts of love is what I think of when I'm with you.
I was so lost and I didn't know which was to turn.
So in love for it helped me to earn, trust
in something that I didn't know a lot about.

So God opened up my understanding and worked
it out for me.

Now I am tickled by love.
Sitting at new heights in my life.
I needed to be thinking of a love that can uplift me,
ignite me, and excite me.

To be ticked by love has me in great hops of being
Forever happy and joyous in life.
To share love with that special someone really makes life
worthwhile and it will make you smile.
To be tickled by love, the pain from all the laughter
we shared.
Thank you for always being there and showing that you cared
to be tickled by love.

© "LOVE NEVER STOPPING" ©
by Nira M. Saleh

I see love never stopping.
But to forever increase, it is what we need.

I see love gone beyond the heavens.
Love gone beyond the next level.

I see love breaking boundaries.
Love beyond the sky.
For it is in our nature to have love for someone
or for something.

I see love never stopping for it will be
like Folgers, "good down to the last drop".
I see love never stopping
For I see love breaking the chains in bondage.
The chains are being broken in limitations.

In love, I see love never stopping.
But forever to increase by measures that cannot be weighed.
Trust in it. It won't be delayed.
And you will be okay.

© "TO GET TO THIS POINT IN LOVE" ©
by Nira M. Saleh

We had a lot of paths that we had to cross.
And in it all, it took much grace and mercy to get to this point
in love.

I'm so glad about it love. So good I can shout
about it. Rejoice in the Lord, for it was well overdue.
Thoughts of changing for the better I knew
that it was all because of you. You see, it took much prayer,
trusting, and believing in God that He would make a way.
So on this day our hearts and spirits are renewed.

To increase in love, life, joy, peace,
In God, in unity, in faith and in all that we seek from God
above, it took the desire to get to this point in love.

In which the world is in the need of, it pushed us
forward and for greatness.
It allowed us to be greater for the love of thee to
get to this point in love.

© "GOING HIGHER IN LOVE" ©
by Nira M. Saleh

We have passed through a lot of obstacles.
We have had a lot of victories won because my love, I'm not
stopping until I'm done.

This love situation has increased and I pray that it never
decrease. In respect or in other ways.
My love, you make my day so new.

I acknowledge that we are going higher in love
Until we reach the sky or until we reach the heavens above.
My love, I declare that we are going higher in love.

It changed us for the better.
It lasted through the storms of weather.
However, do you see it? It shines like the sun.
It has me on a natural high.
Do you feel where I'm coming from?

Because we are going higher in love sent straight from above.
Most of all, one of God's gifts.
A gift of love descending down like doves.
This must be true that we are going   higher in love.

© "A SHARED MOMENT" ©
by Nira M. Saleh

We have shared a lot of thoughts
Not just on things we bought, but sweet memories written down
in history.

Shared between you and me. Oh, how you embraced me with a
time in space that words can never taste the flavor of this
season. Because you being in my life was the reason why every
moment was unforgettable was most of the time incredible for
this is our shared moment.

We laughed.
We cried.
Yes, we also had our differences, but we continued to grow on
each other until we sometimes can tell what each other is about
to say.

For this is a shared moment that took time to get to this point in
our relationship. And baby, I would not have it any other way
than to share this moment with you.

This is our shared moment.
We climbed the highest mountain.
We have crossed the deepest valley.
Baby, I love you and thank you for sharing this time with me.
A shared moment.

© "OH! REALLY BABY?" ©
by Nira M. Saleh

Getting ready for a special event and
everything was in place.
The right outfit, the right shoes, the right perfume.
Everything was good down to the tee, and my love is staring
like WOW, you look amazing!
And I'm looking at him like, Oh! Really Baby?

He said, "Baby you are glowing tonight. I said, Oh! Really
Baby? You think so?
He said, "I know so because you are the center of joy.
Baby I love you and my response was, "Baby you are the center
of my joy, also.

He says, tonight let's forget about everything else. Let's enjoy
it so…we did enjoy every moment at the event
and afterwards.   The next morning he is cooking breakfast
and singing. And, I'm like, Oh! Really Baby?
He stared into my eyes and said, look what God has blessed me
with, a woman of God, and I'm like, Oh! Really Baby?

© "LORD, I'M LOOKING FOR A TURNAROUND" ©
by Nira M. Saleh

Lord, I'm looking for a turnaround within me that

will make you proud, Oh Lord. I'm looking

for a turnaround in my mind, heart, body, and spirit, Oh Lord.

I'm looking to grow spiritually in faith. I ask that you will help

me to increase in you, Oh Lord, and decrease in myself

because if I decrease in myself, there would be room

to grow in Jesus, Oh Lord!

I truly want to be used of God so that the glory of God

will be glorified through your holy name, Oh Lord!

I'm looking for a turnaround that will shake the Devil's

playground. I want to be unstoppable through the spirit of the

Lord. I want to grow stronger in all areas of my life.

Help me to stay in your holy will.

Dear Lord, I'm looking for a turnaround,

not only for me but for the world to see.

And, most of all, for you, Oh Lord!

© "HAND COVERED HEART" ©
by Nira M. Saleh

We are just looking at one another
And yes, I must admit the more I look at you,
The more I just want to hold you in my arms and squeeze you
tight, and don't let go until the morning light.

I don't know what went wrong in that last relationship before
me, and neither is that my concern Honey. I'm just worried
about this one, in how I can learn and be right with you.

Give me your hand and you take mine.
Can I place my hand over your heart and you place your hand
over my heart?
Now we have 2 hands covered hearts
2 gether
4 ever
Hopefully, that is my dream.
Oh, how love carried me
Truly indeed it was there when nothing else was there.

As we look beyond the things we had to cross
together to victory. It's okay because we made it
that's all I wanted from the start
our love is a working process
2 hands covered hearts.

© "LOVE IS NOT TOO FAR AWAY" ©
by Nira M. Saleh

Love is not too far away.
For when you think of love, what do you say or do?

It makes me smile, happy, and overjoyed.
I am truly blessed and I know that love is not too far away.

For God's love and God's grace and mercy is showed toward us
each and every day. So trust, believe, and obey.

Love will have you overwhelmed and you will feel delighted.
It will have you so excited.
When you feel all alone and no one understands or even cares,
please know that God is always there. Yes, He cares.

You need to remember that love is not too far away. This is
something that I must remember and carry with me day-after-
day.

Just remember that love is on its way.
Love Is Not Too Far Away

© "TO BELIEVE IN LOVE" ©
by Nira M. Saleh

To believe in love and that great heart racing, daydreaming,
butterflies in the stomach feeling, and all the
joy that it brings is my everything.

To believe in love when you cannot do anything else but
believe in love comes from God who sits in the Heaven above.

It can make you whole again.
It can heal a wounded heart.
It's what we all need.

To believe in love
To let love take its course and there will be no remorse.
I say, So, give me more.
To Believe In Love.

© "SECOND CHANCE AT LOVE" ©
by Nira M. Saleh

Being in love once before.

And now thinking that love has closed its doors.

But I know that God has more in-store for me.

I know that I must hold on, wait, and see how God can work it
out for me.

God I thank you truly in advance, for I know you have all
power in your hands.

Even before it happens again for me, I know that it awaits for
me. And, I will know that this is my second chance at love.

© "THE DESIRE TO GROW IN LOVE" ©
by Nira M. Saleh

The longing to show live and to express it to the best of our
ability. A love that helped us to grow in unity, it makes us into
such beautiful beings.

Love can help us to grow in a way of maturity that can be
noticed between you and me.

The desire to grow in love takes us to a level of expectancy.
It's something to look forward to. It will keep us on the edge of
our seats wondering what's next what to think.

But God has put in us all the gifts of love with the desire to
grow in love. It has tested our faith, but God was always there
to lead and guide the way.
The desire to grow in love will keep us in a place of peace.

Fulfillment in life
to express it
to show it
to know it
to believe in it
to feel it
the need of it
the desire to grow in love forever and always.

"LOVE CARRIED US ALL THE WAY" ©
by Nira M. Saleh

Testing of all time through the heart of mine
Never imagined that I would find a secret place in love.
For love carried us all the way.
Never to stop praying and hoping that it would
be good down to the last drop.

Love carried us all the way. So if I have to shed a tear,
It will not be in fear because of your love.
It is near only from Thee, my dear.

So hold your head up high and smile because you have
something special in your corner. So there not much to say, but
remember that it was love that carried
us all the way!

© **"JUST ONE MORE CHANCE"** ©
by Nira M. Saleh

So many mistakes wondering which road to take.
So what do I say, my love. We must go on.
Be inspired by love.
Look into my eyes and what do you see?
A cry, a hunger that's trying to reach out to you in the best way
possible.

We shared a lot to call in and quit.
So let's go back and rediscover what it is we lack.

In this relationship on both parts, we maybe didn't give it all we
had.
We just grew bitter. Let's not die in this mess. For God looks
upon the just and the unjust.

Let's make up and forget about the rest, my love.
I just need one more chance to bring something brand new to
the table.

Let's think outside the box.
Let's get back to loving.
I just need one more chance to rekindle this love romance.
Let's take this love hand-by-hand now.
So, let's dance.
Just One More Chance.

© "LET'S GET BACK TO LOVE" ©
by Nira M. Saleh

My Love, I hope that all your fantasies come true,
only for you. This is no longer a dream.
Baby, speak to me. I want to feel you next to me.
I want you to breathe me. The Love box has a lot of roles
which one will you play? Husband and wife,
Mistress and secret lovers, the choice is yours. There is
so many to choose from and etc., but whatever gets your
heart to beating, "yes, it's what I'm seeking!

My love, this for real. We have done all the talking and we
have done all the foreplay. Now, hold my hand
and tell me that it is okay, wait, wait, baby you are worth the
wait. You touch me here and I will touch me here
and I will touch you there.

The beast stepped out of man and he said, "You can touch me
anywhere, but the Love Box.
Because if you enter, there will be a caution sign stating
"ENTER", if you dare, so, please beware.

And tell that special love that if they're good, they are stuck
with you. Baby, I'm not that easy to cut loose, but if this is not
your destination, you can leave, if you choose.
It's not like I have some type of voodoo over you. So let's do
what we must do. This is done all in the name of love and all
because of you.
And, NO, I'm not playing! Do you hear the words I am saying?
There will be a request for more.
But, can you blame it? The Love Box is who to blame.
A love so sweet, tender, and heated. It will have you calling
your lover's name.

© "THE JOY IN THE LORD" ©
by Nira M. Saleh

God didn't promise

that every day was going to be sunny

days, but He did promise that we shall overcome any

obstacle that may be troubling us in the spirit. For the Lord will

give us strength to endure until the end.

And in any situation, we can get through

any test, trial, or tribulation.

For we shall find the Joy in the Lord.

© "LEARNING TO LEAN ON LOVE" ©
by Nira M. Saleh

When you are restless and you don't know what to do,
You might ask yourself what direction to turn to?
Then I think of you for I am learning to lean on love when it
seems like I will fall, but I must remind myself that
God was there through it all.

Also through the support of others, I'm finding out what life
has to offer and what it is all about.
I have faith that things will work out.
I'm learning to lean love to get to that place
that I need to be.

For once now I can imagine me.
All because I am learning to lean on love.
If I have faith in it, it will grow.
If I walk in it, it will sow.
And when it happens, I will know for
I am learning to lean on love.

© "SAVING THE BEST FOR LAST" ©
by Nira M. Saleh

I will save the best for last

As God helps us to get through our past.

And yes, the time passed by fast.

I know that love and faith in God will help us get through

Any hard task.

Always remember to save the best for last.

Savor the moment.

Hold on to precious memories shared between you and me.

Let's hold on to love completely for eternity.

© "MY EVERYTHING" ©
by Nira M. Saleh

You are My Everything!
You are My Everything!
You make my heart sing, my love.
You bring joy to me, can't you see?

It's growing more and more in you and me, my love.
My love express yourself to me. Don't be afraid to let go
and let your feelings show.
Then you will know that you would feel better, if you just let
go,
my everything.

I think about you early in the morning, all through
The day, and all through the night, my love.
You have me flying higher than a kite and I want you to know
that your live is more than alright, my love.

My Everything!
My Everything!
You bring joy to me.
You make my heart sing a sweet melody, you see.
You keep proving how much you love me, my love.

My Everything!
Other than God, my love, you have my heart.
And, I wish that this love won't ever depart, my love.
My Everything!

© "EACH MOMENT THAT I SPEND WITH YOU" ©
by Nira M. Saleh

At the beginning of dawn
And another morning's dew, my love.
I just enjoy spending each moment with you.
For each day is different and brand new.

It's special
It's incredible
It's what I have waited for all my life.

Just to feel the oneness with you, my love
helps me to show, live, and express the love I have for you.
Each moment I spend with you is like a cool breeze
after being in the sun. We have been through every kind of
test, so, I know that victory is won, my love.

What have you done to me to make me feel this way?
Honey, let's celebrate us for our time is well spent,
Not easily broken on the trails of this world.
But to focus on what really matters to us.
Each moment I spend with you, I realize how truly blessed I am
to have you by my side.
We ask that God would lead us and be our daily guide.

In love and in every situation that arises towards and against us,
we will make it through. For God's light
will always be shining through
and this love is especially for you.
Each moment that I spend with you.

© "WEAK FOR LOVE" ©
by Nira M. Saleh

Thinking of you I get so excited that I just

cannot hide it, my love.

My sweetie, come closer to thee, I need to tell you something.

If you are gone from me far too long, my mind will start to

wonder all night long.

When we are together my heart sings a happy song

all the day long, my love.

For you I wait patiently just to hear from you.

I feel myself getting weak that I cannot speak, my love.

© "A SPECIAL LOVE" ©
by Nira M. Saleh

A Special Love
A Special Love
Signed, sealed, and delivered especially for me.

Ascending from the heavens as the angels worship and praise
God. Giving grace and mercy for He knows all about
This "Love Story".

God created us to have love, to show love, and to walk in love.
Something so amazing that it can make your heart sing
A melody deep down in your soul.
Baby, we are talking about the real thang, baby.
It can be bold, sweet, humble, or loud.

A Special Love
It's delightful
It's wonderful
It's special
It's long lasting and enduring.

Each relationship has its own level of special love.
It cannot be measured only showed, expressed,
or talked and texted.
To feel the fulfillment of love grows deeper with time.
And I thank God that I have mine – A Special Love.

© "UNTITLED (WAITING ON LOVE)" ©
by Nira M. Saleh

Darling, we have been at it for hours just staring at each other.
We're wanting to kiss and hug but wait baby, it's too soon.
My mind is telling me no, but my heart and body are saying,
girl, you are about to explode!

We laughed, we talked, we have even gone on long walks
together holding hands. I want to be your lady
and I want you to be my man, baby. Please hear me out.
I don't want to scream and shout without reason. Tell me what
do you believe in?

My love, do you believe in true love?
Do you believe that it can carry you through the test of all time?
Do you believe that it can be heaven sent and divine?
If you ask me do I believe in this, my answer would be YES, I
do believe in something so beautiful that it is worth the wait.

But, wait!
Maybe it's too soon to define this as love, but that's what I
want and needed truly.

Let's wait and see if this love thang
can work out for you and me.

© "LET IT GO" ©
by Nira M. Saleh

All the time spent with you each day gets better
of course, because of you I have learned
to just let it go and to release some of this love
bottled inside of me.

Because the more I let it go, the closer we get and are
becoming, my love.
You bring out another side in me on Cloud 9 and I
don't want to come down.
If only I could stay at this point in my life
forever, my love.
Some people are afraid to let it go.
But only if they knew that it is like a natural high,
really it is!
So just remember to just let it go.
We were created to walk in love.
To show love.
To share love.
To talk about love.
And to express love.
So just let it go.

© "UNTITLED" ©
by Nira M. Saleh

Your love helped me to get back on my feet.
Now, ain't that sweet?
Love beyond another love of this is more than a thought
Emotion, or feeling because you, Oh Lord, bring healing from
deep within.

To places I have been, Lord, free me from all sin.
Rather, it's my thoughts, actions, or spoken words.
Lord, please take this token of praise and let it connect with
your Holy Spirit.

Dear Lord, let it sound like the strings of the cord.
What's more to say but I love you, Dear Lord.

© "UNTITLED (HEY, HEY)" ©
by Nira M. Saleh

Hey, Hey!
What do you say?
I hope and pray that you had a blessed day.

Hey, my love, my darling, my sweetie.
Do you hear me when you are with me?
It's like a dread to me.
I feel uplifted and more gifted.
Empowered, inspired, head over heels in love for you.
This is what you do for me.
You give me joy and life is delightful.
It's so beautiful when you hug and kiss me.
I feel all warm inside, my love.
My heart beats like a drum.
Do you feel where I'm coming from?

My love, My love!
Help me to see the beauty in life. Not so much
about who's wrong or who's right, my love.
You keep that love thang tight, my love.

You and only you are all I will be thinking of, my love.
Your words are sweet and kind, baby.
So many thoughts run through my mind,
I know you're busy.
So I left this message, my love,

Hey, Hey!
I love you today and forever more.

© "HONEY BEE" ©
by Nira M. Saleh

Honey Bee, Honey Bee!
Oh how are thee, my Honey Bee.
I feel safe around thee.
Come closer to the, my Honey Bee.
You woo me, you caress me and even in times you
press me.
In a cloth of your love and affection, I can
Feel the power wave from every direction.
My sweet Honey Bee, you're like a cold glass of water
on a hot summer's day.
I'm not worried about the sweat. So, that ain't even a
threat as long as I don't get over heated and feel
defeated.
When your attention is all I needed.
Honey Bee, Honey Bee!
Oh, where did your sweetness come from?
I'm thinking maybe you were specially created and
designed
Just for me.
My sweet Honey Bee, oh how I love thee.
Oh, how I love thee this moment in time is unique.
And one of a kind, a love so intense and Heavenly
Divine.
Oh, my sweet Honey Bee.
Each hour, minute, second with you is a warm embrace.
My Honey Bee, I can't wait to see your face.
My Sweet Honey Bee!

© "MY SWEETNESS" ©
by Nira M. Saleh

My sweetness, my sweetness!
Tell me where you have been because I've been waiting all day
just to see your face.
My sweetness, my sweetness!
Do you realize how much I missed you baby? Really! Okay.

My sweetness!
You are sweeter than pure sugar.
You are sweeter than honey.
Yes, I really love you, baby.

I'm not worried about your money.
You see, I look for what's in the heart of a man.
Can't you understand in return I hope that you love me
for who I am and don't care about what
others got to say about me?

I am going to be me. Love it or not.
I will not pretend just to get what you got.
Because that's messed up.
I am not going to play with your feelings.
This is real!

My sweetness!
I've had enough of games. So in return, I hope
you feel the same.
My sweetness!
I love you and I care about you, and I hope
you feel the same way about me.
My sweetness!

© "CRUISE ON LOVE" ©
by Nira M. Saleh

If love was a cruise on a special boat, I would
stay there waiting for just the smooth sail
across the lakes, oceans, and seas.

Once I reach the shore I would pull back and tell the captain
"the ride of love, just once more".
Then again off to the waters sailing deep without
a care in the world.
Forgetting all the problems behind,
but to delight in this joy of mine.

Let's cruise together off until the sun sets. Maybe later
we can listen to Keith Sweat, take a drink of wine,
and hold you from behind.
No more waiting, now you are mine to love.
Days and nights to remember from January to December.
In and out of time once more.
I say you are mine.

If I could I would stay on this cruise boat with you.
Loving you whenever, however, whatever just to show you how
deep my love flows.
Now, it's been days we have reached the shore.
Now, today, and forever I take your hand to tell you,
you are the one whom my heart adores.

© "LOOK AT US" ©
by Nira M. Saleh

Look at us! Together holding hands going in unity as we take a
stand for God, for peace and in the name of love.

Look at us! Sharing precious quality time
designed for you and me.
We must remember that in love apples don't fall far
from the tree.
You see how love was there from the beginning.
And with love, we are winning.

Look at us!
Shining like stars in the night sky, it has us on a
super natural high.
You don't ever have to wonder why because
real love is what we got.

Look at us!
Growing in unity,
Growing in good hopes
Growing in good wishes.
For that's what I'm speaking of.
Look at us!

© "LET'S TAKE A TOAST" ©
by Nira M. Saleh

Let's take a toast for love.

To love and to have love, true love.

At heart and not knowing where it start.

But I'm thankful that it is here

So let's go about our way, My Dear.

Loving life to the fullest I will never get tired of it.

I will live it, grow in it, breathe it, and show it.

Let's take a toast for love.

© "I GOT IT BAD FOR YOU" ©
by Nira M. Saleh

From the rising of the moon to the rising of the sun
without you, my life is done.
I can't even picture a day without you.
You turn my sky from gray to blue
With you I will remain faithful and true,
because no one loves me like you do.

If I could move mountains for you, I would just
want to see your face again.
Only with you a new life will begin.
I got it bad for you, my love.

Ascending into the air like a dove free from bondage.
But at the same time a symbol of purity,
love, and affection.
I was so hopeless right until love pointed in
your direction.
I love you without a cause.
For you time paused.
I got it bad for you.

© "AMAZED AT LOVE" ©
by Nira M. Saleh

Amazed at love.
How I matured in it, walk in it.
Believe in it and at times I have reached the highest point in it.

It has changed me and I know for a fact it has
helped me to grow.

I don't care about who knows,
so I am determined to let it show

I am so amazed at love for it can be expressed
quietly or out loud.
But those memories will keep you.

A feeling that make you proud, so stand now
and claim your share.
Staring love in the eyes and we know that it would be there
to hold us in those times. We may feel weak
for it will grab you by the hand and help you to stand
on your feet.
Arise
Arise
Arise

© "SAVING THE BEST FOR LAST" ©
by Nira M. Saleh

I will save the best for last

As God helps us to get through our past.

And yes, the time passed by fast.

I know that love and faith in God will help us get through

Any hard task.

Always remember to save the best for last.

Savor the moment.

Hold on to precious memories shared between you and me.

Let's hold on to love completely for eternity.

.

Author Contact

Miss Nira Saleh

606 Gilliland Street

Kosciusko, Mississippi 39090

Phone: 662-792-0012

Additional copies of this book and other titles
form C&C Publishing are available on Amazon,
local bookstores and websites.

C&C Publishing

606 Gilliland Street

Kosciusko, Mississippi 39090